TITUS IN TROUBLE

By James Reeves

Illustrated by

Edward Ardizzone

THE BODLEY HEAD · LONDON · SYDNEY · TORONTO

SBN 370 00709 3

Printed in Great Britain for
The Bodley Head Ltd
9 Bow Street, London WC2 E 7AL
by A & M Weston Ltd., South Wigston
Set in Monotype Plantin
First published 1959
Second edition 1969
Reprinted 1971

TITUS lived in London in a narrow street beside the River Thames. It was a hundred years ago and more. There were sailing ships on the water right at the end of the street. Titus wanted to go to sea, and the master of one of the ships had promised to take him as cabin boy on his next voyage. But a dreadful thing happened.

One day Titus went into Mr. Busby's curiosity shop to have a look round. He often went there in search of telescopes and ships in bottles. Mr. Busby did not mind, so long as he broke nothing. But to-day he was unlucky. Reaching up to take hold of an old ship's compass, he lost his balance and stepped back into a table laden with china and glass. A pair of tall vases crashed to the ground and broke in pieces.

Mr. Busby was furious.

'I'm sorry, sir,' said Titus. 'I hope they aren't too valuable.'

'They aren't *now*,' said the shopkeeper. 'But before you sent them flying, you clumsy young fool, they were worth every penny of fifteen pounds. I tell you what, though. Seeing you're only a nipper, I'll let you off with ten. Just you run home and bring me the money as soon as you can.'

Titus was too dazed to tell Mr. Busby that he hadn't a penny in the world. He said he would get the money as soon as he could, and left the shop. Where was a boy like him to get ten pounds? Some boys are good at mending things. Titus only seemed able to break them. There was nothing for it. He would have to go to work to pay for the broken

china. Until he had done that, he could not think of going to sea.

'I shall get ten shillings a week,' he thought to himself. That was a lot of money in those days. As he strode uphill

towards the City, he sang a song he had learnt from his father:

'Were you ever off Cape Horn
Where it's always fine and warm?
See the lion and the unicorn
Riding on a donkey!

'Hey ho! and away we go,
Donkey riding, donkey riding,
Hey ho! and away we go,
Riding on a donkey!'

Presently Titus found himself at the door of a great warehouse. He went boldly up to the manager, and said he wanted work.

'Right-o, sonny,' said the manager. 'I'll give you seven shillings a week, and you can start straight away.'

So Titus got his first job. It wasn't so bad to begin with,

P. SMI
BOTT

but soon the gloomy factory made him sad, and he wished he was down by the river. The smell of the pickles made him feel sick—for that was what the place was, a pickle factory.

Sometimes he carried the jars to the trolleys, sometimes he stuck the labels on. But whatever he did, by the end of the first week he was wishing he could do something else. Only

one thing made him happy—he broke nothing. He dared not.

At twelve o'clock on Saturday, Titus was given his first week's pay, and set off proudly homewards. Then he saw an old woman selling oranges on the quay. The sight of the golden fruit made him thirsty.

'How much?' he asked.

'Tell you what, dearie,' answered the old woman. 'Mind my basket for ten minutes while I go and get myself a bite to eat, and you can have a couple for nothing.'

Titus sat down by the basket, which was perched on the wall at the edge of the quay. Nobody came to buy oranges, and Titus looked at the seagulls circling round the masts.

Suddenly a great white sail appeared in the distance. Titus jumped up to get a better view, and as he did so he knocked into the basket. The golden oranges rolled over the edge and bounded and tumbled into the river. Titus clutched at the basket and managed to save it, but most of the oranges had gone.

Just then the woman came back.

'What are you doing, you young demon?' she cried. 'Just look at my beautiful oranges—all gone to feed the fishes!'

Poor Titus had to give her five shillings of his week's money to buy some more fruit. So she gave him one to eat, and he went home slowly and sadly, with hardly enough heart to suck his orange.

Next Monday Titus decided not to go back to the pickle factory. As he wandered along the street, he came to a printer's shop. Here, a printer was making copies of songs and ballad-sheets, to be sold in the streets for a halfpenny or a penny each. As Titus stopped at the open door, he

happened to be singing his favourite song:

'Hey ho! and away we go,
Donkey riding, donkey riding—'

'So you likes a song, does you?' said the printer. 'How'd it be if you was to sing some of these in the streets, and see how many you can sell?'

'I'll try,' said Titus.

'Good,' said the printer. 'Take a bundle of these, and when you sees folks standing about on the corners or in the market, you starts to sing. I'll give you sixpence a day and a penny extra for every dozen you sell.'

So Titus set off, and presently stopped in an open place and began singing as best he could. He soon learned two or three ballads, and people stopped to listen to his young, clear voice. The passers-by, especially the ladies, were not slow to buy his sheets. Soon he had sold all his stock, so he went

back to the printer for more.

For a whole week Titus went his rounds, singing and selling ballads till his throat ached.

At first the weather was fine, but on the last day of the week a storm blew up; just as Titus was turning a corner, a

sudden gust of wind and rain caught his bundle of songs and carried them all away, up the street and over the roof-tops. Some went fluttering down into the street, where they were trampled under foot. Not more than half a dozen could be saved.

The printer took all Titus' wages to pay for the lost ballad-sheets. This made Titus so angry that he went back there no more.

'How shall I ever make ten pounds?' he said to himself. 'I can't even make ten pence.'

The next job Titus got was in a big store where they sold suits for gentlemen, dresses for ladies, and stuff for making coats and frocks. Titus was a messenger-boy. He carried parcels up and down stairs, and ran errands for the manager and the assistants. The manager was an important person called Mr. Carmichael. He looked down his nose at Titus and at everybody else. He went about as if he hoped to be made Lord Mayor.

One day Titus was sent from the top of the shop to the ground floor with a huge roll of red satin. Just as he came to the top of the stairs, he tripped. Clasping the end of the stuff with one hand and the bannisters with the other, he saved himself from falling; but the roll careered away down the long staircase, just as if it were being laid out for the Queen! The assistants and the customers were almost as surprised as Titus. Then something even more extraordinary happened. Mr. Carmichael was at that very moment about to go down the stairs. He was speaking importantly to someone behind

him. As he put his foot on the top step, he slipped on the satin and fell. He could not save himself, but went slithering right down to the ground floor. A cry of horror went up from the assistants, who had never before seen their manager in such a dreadful situation. But the customers were delighted, and roared with laughter.

Titus did not wait to hear what Mr. Carmichael would say. He took himself out of the building as fast as he could run.

Titus decided to have one more try at earning some money.

'*Hey ho! and away we go*,' he chanted as he strode off towards the big railway station. Surely he could find work there! When he arrived, an express train was about to start

for Scotland. Porters were pushing barrows to and fro. Passengers were leaning out of the windows. Friends and relations were pulling out handkerchiefs. Suddenly the guard waved his green flag and blew a piercing blast on his whistle. The engine gave a great roar, and the last door was slammed shut.

Then a man in a check overcoat ran on to the platform carrying two huge bags. He almost knocked Titus off his feet.

'Here, boy!' he said. 'Take one of these. Quick, follow me!'

Titus seized the bag that was thrust at him, and the man

wrenched open the door of a compartment just as the train began to move. He threw the bag he was carrying on to a seat and grabbed one handle of the other. Titus, still holding on tight, was hauled into the carriage. A porter slammed the door.

'I've got to get out!' shouted Titus.

'Too late!' called the porter.

Titus was in the carriage being taken away faster and faster every moment.

'Sorry, boy,' said the man in the check coat. 'Should have let go, you know. Only thing to do is to wait till we get to a station. Then you can take the next train back to London.'

On and on they went into the green countryside. Presently the train stopped. They had come to a level-crossing, and the gates were shut. A donkey pulling a cartload of vegetables was in the very middle of the track, and refused to move. So the man at the level-crossing had had to signal the train to halt.

'Now's your chance,' said the man in the check coat. 'Hop out here. Get back home as best you can. Here's five shillings for you. Dash my whiskers, what a lark!'

He opened the door, and Titus jumped down and made for the road. He had no idea where he was, but he could see the roofs of houses and a church spire in the distance.

Soon he came to a big house at the end of a drive. A huge van was drawn up in front of it, and Titus could see that men were carrying furniture out and stowing it in the van. Two great horses were in the shafts, quietly munching from their nosebags. Titus felt hungry. He went boldly up the steps of the house, and was going to ring the bell when a lady came

out carrying a bird-cage with a canary in it. She was crying and dabbing her eyes with a handkerchief.

'Ruined!' she said. 'Quite, quite ruined! Yet they must be somewhere! They must, they must.'

'Emmeline, Emmeline,' said a kind-looking gentleman who had come up behind her, carrying a set of croquet hoops and six mallets, 'don't take on so, my dear. We've looked everywhere. There's nothing more to be done. Let us make the best of things.'

'Oh, Augustus,' wailed the lady, 'to think it should come to this! If only our aunt had told us where she hid them. But she was always a dark horse, and now she no longer lives to tell us.'

Titus couldn't imagine what was going on. He only knew that he was hungry.

'Please,' he said, 'if you would give me something to eat, perhaps I could find them—whatever they are that this dark horse has hidden.'

'My boy,' said the gentleman, 'I fear you can do nothing, but by all means have something to eat—that is, if there *is*

anything. My sister and I, as you see, are moving house. Our furniture is going to be sold, and we shall have to live in shabby seaside lodgings. We have had to give up this beautiful house, all because our aunt died without telling us what she did with the family jewels.'

'I expect she sold them,' said Emmeline. 'But what is that to you, boy? Come into the house and I will find you some food. Afterwards, perhaps you'll help us carry our things to this pantechnicon.'

Titus was given some bread and cheese, a few grapes, and

a glass of milk. Then he helped to take things out to the van.

It was a sad sight, all the fine furniture and carpets being packed away to be carted off and sold. Titus began to feel as sad as the poor lady and gentleman.

'Here, my lad,' said one of the removal men, 'give us a hand with this.'

He was holding one end of a chest of drawers. Titus lifted the other end, and followed the man down the steps. He couldn't see where he was going, but managed to reach the bottom without falling. The man climbed on to the tail of the van still holding the chest. He called to Titus to steady it below, but alas! Titus could hold it no longer. The chest

toppled backwards and crashed on to the ground.

'Now you've gone and done it!' said the man.

At the sound of the crash, the kind gentleman and his sister ran down the steps. Titus knelt on the ground and tried to raise the fallen chest. It was badly broken. Then he saw something on the stones. Quickly he picked it up. It was a package wrapped in tissue-paper, which had burst open. Titus lifted out something bright and shining. It was a diamond necklace! Inside the package were more jewels—rubies, pearls, and other precious stones. The crash must have broken open a false bottom in one of the drawers, and the family treasures were at last revealed.

'Oh, what a wonderful thing!' cried the gentleman, pressing the jewels into Emmeline's trembling hands. 'What a happy accident! My dear boy, come inside and have some more bread and cheese. Have some champagne! Have anything there is!'

There is little more to tell. Everyone went into the house—

Augustus and Emmeline, Titus and the removal men—and as splendid a feast was provided as was possible in the circumstances. Afterwards the men took all the furniture back into the house. The lady and gentleman, their fortunes restored, gave Titus fifteen pounds as a reward for his happy accident.

Titus was so pleased that he hardly knew what to say; but he thanked them warmly, and everyone said good-bye amid laughter and tears of joy. A cab took Titus to the station, where he bought a ticket for London. He was on his way back to where the big ships lay peacefully at anchor in the still water of the River Thames. The handsome reward was

safely tucked away in his inside pocket.

'Now I'll be able to pay back the ten pounds I owe for breaking those vases,' he said to himself. 'After that, it's off to sea I go!'

And sitting back in his corner seat, Titus began to sing joyfully to himself:

'Were you ever in Cardiff Bay
Where the folks all shout Hooray!
Here comes Jack with his three months' pay,
Riding on a donkey!

'Hey ho! and away we go,
Donkey riding, donkey riding,
Hey ho! and away we go,
Riding on a donkey!'